This sakhi book belongs to:

....

This book was devised, designed and completed by volunteers from
Sikh History And Religious Education (S.H.A.R.E.)

Illustrations by Cristian Rodriguez.

Published by Sikh History and Religious Education

Registered Charity Number: 1120428

Khalsa@sharecharityuk.com

H A R E

Dedicated to all the powerful and inspiring sisters out there...

Your strength and mothering nature contributes to upstanding individuals in society.

This is a book all about <u>Bebe Nanaki Jee</u>. She was <u>Guru Nanak Dev Jee</u>'s older sister. Bebe Nanaki Jee was very special.

She taught us how to be good <u>Sikhs</u>.

Bebe Nanaki Jee was born in 1464 in her maternal town of Chahal, present day Lahore.

Her mother was Mata Tripta Jee and her father was Metha Kalu Jee.

Bebe Nanaki loved to hear stories about God. She would sit with her mother for hours listening and asking questions about the <u>Lord</u>.

When Bebe Nanaki was 5 years old, her brother Nanak was born. Nanak didn't cry like the other children. This was Bebe Nanaki's first clue that her little brother was special.

Nanak never enjoyed playing games with the other children. Instead, he enjoyed discovering God's creation, such as flowers, trees and animals. Bebe Nanaki Jee would watch Nanak lovingly.

She would hear her brother say "He is here! He is here!". She knew that her brother was different from the other children.

When Nanak's father would get upset with Him, Bebe Nanaki Jee would protect Nanak and never let her father harm Him.

Bebe Nanaki Jee was married to <u>Jai Ram Jee</u> in 1475.

She went to live with her husband in <u>Sultanpur</u>, leaving her brother behind in <u>Talwandi</u>.

Nanak was never interested in making lots of money. He would give all His money to the poor or <u>Saintly</u> people.

Metha Kalu Jee would get very upset with Nanak, so Bebe Nanaki Jee suggested that her brother came and lived with her.

Whilst living in Sultanpur, Nanak made friends with all the townspeople.

After a while, His friend, <u>Bhai Mardana Jee</u>, came to stay with Him.

One <u>Amrit Vela</u>, whilst having His <u>Ishnaan</u>, Nanak disappeared.

When Bhai Mardana Jee realised Nanak was nowhere to be seen, he hurried to tell Bebe Nanaki Jee.

The townspeople searched for Nanak day and night but eventually gave up, believing He had drowned.

Bebe Nanaki Jee, however, knew that Nanak had not drowned and she waited for 3 days at the riverbank for her brother to return.

When Nanak emerged from the water, Bebe Nanaki Jee fell at His feet and said "You are my Guru and I shall follow you, always."

Bebe Nanaki Jee was the first person to bow to Guru Nanak Dev Jee.

Bebe Nanaki Jee's husband arranged the marriage of Guru Nanak Dev Jee to <u>Mata Sulakani Jee</u>. They had two sons, <u>Lakhmi Das</u> and <u>Sri Chand</u>.

Guru Nanak Dev Jee travelled the world to teach people about God's message of love and respect.

During this time, Bebe Nanaki Jee took care of Mata Sulakani Jee and her two nephews, Lakhmi Das and Sri Chand.

Bebe Nanaki Jee never had any children of her own.

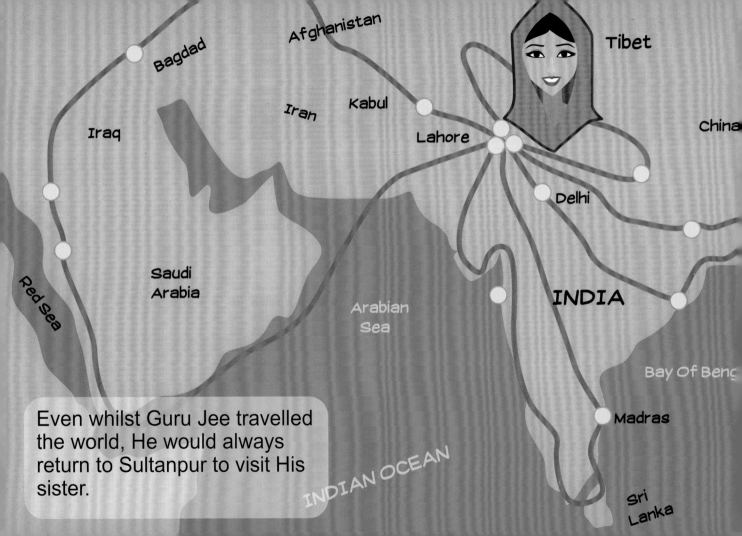

Even whilst Guru Jee travelled the world, He would always return to Sultanpur to visit His sister.

The love that Guru Nanak Dev Jee and Bebe Nanaki Jee had was very special. They respected and cared for each other, as all humans beings should.

Bebe Nanaki Jee never questioned Guru Nanak Dev Jee and His practices. She trusted the Guru with all her heart. We should trust Guru Jee in the same way.

Bebe Nanaki Jee listened to everything Guru Jee asked her to do. We should listen to Guru Jee in the same way.

Bebe Nanaki Jee loved Guru Jee with all her heart and soul. We should love Guru Jee in the same way.

Lets See what you learnt!

1. In which town was Bebe Nanaki born?

_____

2. In which year was Bebe Nanaki's brother Nanak born?

_____

3. Nanak had a friend who came to visit Him. What was Nanak's friend's name?

_____

4. What is the name of the river into which Nanak disappeared for 3 days ?

_____

5. What are the names of Bebe Nanaki Jee's mother and father ?

_____

WELL DONE!

Glossary

Amrit Vela : Amrit—Ambrosial Nector (immortal) Vela—Time
Bebe Nanaki Jee : Eldest sister of the first Guru of the Sikhs
Bhai Mardana Jee : Companion/friend of the first Guru of the Sikhs
Guru : Gu - Dark Ru—light (darkness into Light)
Ishnaan : To bathe in cold water whilst reciting Gods Name
Jai Ram Jee : Husband of Bebe Nanaki Jee
Lakmi Das : Son of Guru Nanak Devi Jee
Mata Sulakani Jee : Wife of Guru Nanak Dev Jee
Mata Tripta Jee : Mother of Guru Nanak Dev Jee
Metha Kalu Jee : Father of Guru Nanak Dev Jee
River Bein : One of the five rivers that flow through the state of Punjab
Saintly : People who are in constant meditation and perform good deeds
Sikh : One who is a follower of Guru Nanak Dev jee, learner, disciple
Sri Chand : Son of Guru Nanak Dev Jee
Sultanpur : Town where Nanak stayed with his sister and met God
Talwandi : Birthplace of Guru Nanak Dev Jee, now present day Nankan Sahib, Pakistan